# SHORT STORY OF KUVEMPU

## KUPPALLI VENKATAPPA PUTTAPPA

CHANDAN S AVANTI IDLOOR

ISBN 979-888503726-6

This Book is Dedicating to my Grandparents

SHRI LATE.CHANNABASAPPA AVANTI IDLOORSMT
LATE.SHIVAMMA AVANTI IDLOOR


Father Shankarlingappa Avanti Idloor

Mother Shivaleela S Avanti Idloor

Thanks to:-

VEERESH S AVANTI IDLOOR

Special Thanks to:-

Who will read this book to them... ♥?♥?♥?❣?❣?❣?

# Contents

# Foreword

Author....

**CHANDAN S AVANTI IDLOOR**

# Preface

CO Author..

VEERESH S AVANTI IDLOOR

# Acknowledgements

Please who will read this book they shoud mail me how is the book.

Email:-melodysingerchandu@gmail.com
Contact:- 8861866493
Contact:-9449818170

# Prologue

YOU ALL PEOPLE SHOULD ENCOURAGE ME TO WRITE MORE BOOKS ABOUT INDIAN FREEDOM FIGHTERS,SCIENTISTS,KARNATAKA SINGERS,ETC

# CHAPTER ONE

# SHORT STORY OF KUVEMPU

**Kuppali Venkatappa Puttappa (29 December 1904 – 11 November 1994),**

popularly known by his pen name Kuvempu was an Indian poet, playwright, novelist and critic.

He is widely regarded as the greatest Kannada poet of the 20th century.

He was the first Kannada writer to receive the Jnanpith Award.

Kuvempu studied at Mysuru University in the 1920s, taught there for nearly three decades and served as its vice-chancellor from 1956 to 1960.

He initiated education in Kannada as the language medium. For his contributions to Kannada Literature, the Government of Karnataka decorated him with the honorific Rashtrakavi ("National Poet") in 1964 and Karnataka Ratna ("The Gem of Karnataka") in 1992.

He was conferred the Padma Vibhushan by the Government of India in 1988. He penned the Karnataka State Anthem Jaya Bharata Jananiya Tanujate.

**Early life and education**

**Kuvempu's ancestral house in Kuppali**

Kuvempu was born in Hirkodige, a village in Koppa taluk of Chikmangalur district and raised in Kuppalli, a village in Shivamogga district of the erstwhile Kingdom of Mysore (now in Karnataka) into to a Kannada-speaking Vokkaliga family.[6] His mother Seethamma hailed from Koppa, Chikmangalur, while his father Venkatappa was from Kuppali, a village in Thirthahalli taluk (in present-day Shimoga district), where he was raised.[9][6] Early in his childhood, Kuvempu was home-schooled by an appointed teacher from South Canara.[citation needed] He joined the Anglo-Vernacular school in Thirthahalli to continue his middle school education. Kuvempu's father died when he was only twelve. He finished his lower and secondary education in Kannada and English languages in Thirthahalli and moved to Mysore for further education at the Wesleyan High School. Thereafter, he pursued college studies at the Maharaja College of Mysore and graduated in 1929, majoring in Kannada.[10]

**Family**

Kuvempu married Hemavathi on 30 April 1937.

He was forced into enter marital life on this faculty out of Ramakrishna Mission.

Kuvempu has two sons, Poornachandra Tejaswi and Kokilodaya Chaitra, and two daughters, Indukala and Tharini.

Tharini is married to K.Chidananda Gowda the former Vice-Chancellor of Kuvempu University.

His home in Mysore is called Udayaravi.

His son Poornachandra Tejaswi was a polymath, contributing significantly to Kannada literature, photography, calligraphy, digital imaging, social movements, and agriculture.

**Career**

Kuvempu began his academic career as a lecturer of Kannada language at the Maharaja's College in Mysore in 1929.

He worked as an assistant professor in the Central college, Bangalore from 1936.

He re-joined Maharaja's college in Mysore in 1946 as a professor.

He went on to become the principal of the Maharaja's college in 1955.

In 1956 he was selected as the Vice-Chancellor of Mysore University where he served till retirement in 1960.

He was the first graduate from Mysore University to rise to that position.

**Kavimane — Kuvempu Memorial**

Kuvempu's memorial in Kavishaila, Kuppali

The childhood home of Kuvempu at Kuppali has been converted into a museum by Rashtrakavi Kuvempu Pratishtana (a trust dedicated to Kuvempu).

This trust has undertaken immense developmental works in Kuppali to showcase Kuvempu and his works to the external world.

On 23 November 2015 night, many valuables including the Padma Shri and Padma Bhushan awards conferred on poet laureate Kuvempu were stolen from Kavimane.

The entire museum has been ransacked. The surveillance cameras there have also been damaged.

The Jnanapith award kept there has remained intact..

**Kavishaila**

The gradually rising hill south of the house is named Kavishaila, Kuvempu's mortal remains were placed at Kavishaila.

iographies on Kuvempu

Kuvempu on a 2017 stamp of India

Annana Nenapu, Poornachandra Tejaswi

Yugada Kavi, K.C. Shiva Reddy

Kuvempu, Pradhan Gurudatta

Magalu Kanda Kuvempu, Tharini Chidananda,
Commemoration

The Kuvempu University in Shimoga, Karnataka was established in 1987.

The Vishwamanava Express was named in honour of Kuvempu's idea of "Vishwa Manava"

("Universal Man").

India Post honoured Kuvempu by releasing a postage stamp in 1997 and 2017.

Birthday: December 29, 1904

Died At Age: 89

Sun Sign: Capricorn

Also Known As: Kuppali Venkatappa Puttappa

Born Country: India

Born In: Chikkamagaluru District

Famous As: Novelist

Poets Novelists

Family:

Spouse/Ex-: Hemavathi

Father: Venkatappa Gowda

Mother: Seethamma

Children: Indukala, Kokilodaya Chaitra, Poornachandra Tejaswi, TariNi

Died On: November 11, 1994

Place Of Death: Mysore

More Facts

Recommended Lists:
Indian Celebrities
Who was Kuvempu?

Kuppali Venkatappa Puttappa, better known as Kuvempu, was an Indian poet, playwright, novelist and critic. He is regarded by many as the best Kannada poet of the 20th century. He was also the first Kannada writer who received the Jnanpith Award. He completed his education from Mysuru University, after which he continued to work there as a teacher. During this time, he contributed to several literary works. His best known works include the epic 'Sri Ramayana Darshanam', based on the famous Hindu epic Ramayana, and novels such as 'Kanuru Heggaditi' (Proprietress of Kanuru). He is credited with writing the Karnataka State Anthem 'Jaya Bharata Jananiya Tanujate.' Throughout his life, he received numerous honors, including the Sahitya Akademi Award, and the Padma Bhushan and Padma Vibhushan, the third and second highest civilian honors in India.

Image Credit

Recommended Lists:

Indian Men

Male Poets

Indian Poets

Male Writers

Career

Kuvempu's academic career started as a lecturer of Kannada language at Maharaja's College in Mysore. Between 1936 and 1946, he worked as an assistant professor in the Central College in Bangalore.

Later in 1946, he again joined Maharaja's College as a professor.

Eventually, he went on to become its principal. In 1956, he was made the vice-chancellor of Mysore University.

He served in this post till his retirement in 1960.

He is also the first graduate from the university who reached that position.

He began composing his literary works in English, with a collection of poems known as 'Beginner's Muse'. Later, he decided to write in his native language, Kannada, instead.

He also led the movement which emphasized Kannada as the medium of education in Karnataka.

He founded the 'Institute of Kannada Studies' in the Mysore University, which was later renamed after him as 'Kuvempu Institute of Kannada Studies'. Throughout his life, he wrote and published twenty-five collections of poems, two novels, as well as biographies and literary criticisms.

He also wrote several collections of stories, essays and a few plays.

His most important works include 'Sri Ramayana Darshana', an epic based on the famous Hindu epic 'Ramayana,' through which he discusses duties, rights as well as the social responsibilities that an individual has.

This work earned him the Sahitya Akademi as well as the Jnanapith award.

He also wrote two novels 'Kanuru Heggaditi', which translates to 'Proprietress of Kanuru' and 'Malegalalli Madumagulu,' which translates to 'The Bride in the Mountains'.

His works were much appreciated and earned him several honors,

the most notable ones being 'Padma Bhushan' in 1958, and 'Padma Vibhushan' in 1988.